Baby, I Love You

Desiree DuBois

Author's Note

Hello lovely reader!

Thank you so much for continuing to follow my spicy Why Choose Romance with this companion to the duology. This book may be small, but it has some strong themes, including exhibitionism, conception, childbirth, analingus (protection used), DPiV, child protective services (no children taken from their parents), past child abuse mentioned. Other than that, I hope you enjoy reading a lot of sex, because there's a lot of it!

I'm Canadian! I chose to use American spellings for the most part, but I kept the Canadian spelling of pyjama. I hope you don't mind my eccentricities.

Childbirth is a unique experience for every person, and the experience contained within is based on that of the author.

Love you all! Mwah!

Desiree DuBois

Part One:

Twister with a Twist

This story takes place during the events of chapter 17 in I Knew I Loved You. *You do not need to read that first, but this is intended as a companion piece.*

Tony shambled down the stairs, rubbing sleep from his eyes. He caught sight of his hair in one of the mirrors in the foyer; it looked like someone had been running their fingers through it. He smirked. They had been. Repeatedly.

Following the scent of bacon and the sounds of other guests into the kitchen, he took a moment to assess the situation before fully entering.

He and his partners, Amanda and James, had accepted Glenn's invitation to Thanksgiving. But not at his house; his parents were in the process of deciding whether to buy a massive mansion on the cape, one that they would be renting out for large gatherings exactly like this one. As part of the buyer's agreement, Glenn had been allowed to invite a huge number of people out to give the house a test run.

They'd arrived yesterday and taken advantage of the unseasonably gorgeous weather on the beach, followed by dinner and party games on the back deck.

Party games that had taken a decidedly sexy turn. Tony grinned to himself as flashes of the evening paraded through his mind.

Despite the relatively early hour and copious amounts of alcohol, about half the guests were awake and playing a game in the sitting room off the kitchen. Loud cheers and laughter punctuated by brief silences intrigued him, but not enough to pull him from the shadowy alcove.

Not yet.

Tony'd never thought of himself as shy, especially not with the streak of exhibitionism that his partners drew out of him, but the idea of approaching a large group of people he didn't know was making him nervous.

"Hey man," Glenn said from behind him, making him jump.

Glenn clapped his hand on Tony's shoulder. "They don't bite," he confided. "Much." He winked.

Tony chuckled. "Yeah, I know. Just nervous to be, you know, out."

"Out?" Glenn pursed his lips. "You mean we weren't supposed to know that you and James were hot for each other?"

Tony flushed. "It's fairly new to us. Especially in public."

"I promise, nobody noticed," Glenn said dryly. "It might have been the first time your lips touched in public without it being a dare, but remember, people saw James swallow your cock down to the root two years ago."

"On a dare," Tony added quickly.

"Uh huh." Glenn raised an eyebrow. "He didn't protest."

"We've always been close," Tony replied weakly.

"Mmhmm," Glenn hummed noncommittally. "I'm glad that you're out now. You're practically glowing."

"Not keeping a massive secret is a huge relief. Who knew?" Tony asked sarcastically.

"The only one you were successful at hiding it from was James himself. And vice versa." Glenn rolled his eyes. "How Amanda didn't knock some sense into the two of you earlier is beyond me."

"She didn't know either." Tony shrugged. "Too close to us, I guess."

"I suppose." Glenn gestured into the kitchen. "After you."

Reluctantly, Tony entered the massive kitchen and grabbed a plate, circling around the warming plates full of breakfast foods.

"They still asleep?" Glenn asked.

"Hmm?" Tony hummed, not fully paying attention to his friend as he heaped his plate with scrambled eggs and bacon. "Oh, yeah, no. Not really. They'll be down shortly." He added a spoonful of crispy potatoes.

"Tired them out?" Glenn asked with a wink.

Trying and failing to hide the grin that followed, Tony inclined his head. "More like my stomach demanded attention."

"You gave up sex for food?" Glenn exclaimed, eyes wide.

"I didn't say anything about giving up sex," Tony replied with a chuckle. "Nosy bastard."

"I am," Glenn replied unrepentantly. "Mostly because you're usually fairly open." His eyes narrowed. "Why aren't you now?"

Tony shrugged. "Because they're not here. I don't talk about sex without them."

"Ahh, I get it." Glenn nodded at the door. "Speak of the devil. Or angel in this case, perhaps."

Amanda and James appeared, both looking disheveled. She immediately went to Tony, plucking a potato off his plate and popping it into her mouth. "Hot," she gasped, mouth open, the potato clenched between her teeth.

James shook his head. "You never learn." He passed her the glass of milk he'd just finished pouring for himself.

Mouth relieved, she snuggled into Tony. "Is that my plate?"

"Nope."

"You sure?" She batted her eyes at him.

Tony chuckled. "Quite sure. I'll save you a seat." He kissed her upturned lips and headed into the sitting room.

There wasn't much space left, but people shifted to make some for him, and he found himself sitting next to Kevin, who they'd recently become reacquainted with.

"How's it going? Sleep okay?" Tony asked before stuffing food in his mouth.

"Oh, yeah, just fine," Kevin said shyly. "I don't feel like I belong here."

Tony nodded encouragingly, hoping Kevin would continue to talk so he wouldn't have to.

Fortunately, Kevin followed the unstated rules of conversation. "There's a lot of flirtation going on amongst the singles," he continued. "I've never had so many girls try to make out with me."

Managing to swallow before he sprayed the other man with masticated food, Tony asked, "And that makes you feel like you don't belong?"

"They don't know me," Kevin protested.

"No, they don't. And yet..." Tony shrugged. "You said 'try to make out'. Does that mean you turned them down?"

"It didn't feel right," Kevin said sheepishly.

"I see." Tony assessed the guy. "Who did you want to ask?"

Kevin flushed, but before he could press, Amanda appeared with her full plate.

"Thanks for saving me a seat," she said, sinking onto Tony's lap. "What are we talking about?"

He rearranged his plate to be able to eat around her. "The person Kevin wants to make out with."

"Oooh!" Amanda wiggled in place and glanced at the faces of the people seated around them. "Let me see if I can guess. Are they awake yet?"

"Shh," Kevin hissed. "I don't want anyone to know!"

Amanda tilted her head, considering him. "Kevin, you're allowed to have fun this weekend. You want to kiss someone, you ask. Hardly anyone says no."

"I did," he groaned. "Three girls last night, after that kissing game."

"That's a compliment," Tony put in.

"Not to them," Kevin said.

"Was one of them the one you wanted?"

"No, but what if they tell her that I'm saying no? Then she'll never ask me!" Kevin exclaimed.

"Valid point." Tony licked the tines of his fork. "Then you'll have to do the asking."

"I couldn't," Kevin said, blanching under his flush.

"What color bracelet is she wearing?" Amanda asked. "Is she available?"

"It's green," Kevin admitted.

"Then she's available. What's the worst that could happen?"

"She says no, and my high school crush fizzles out," he said sadly.

"Aww, high school!" Amanda cooed. "I know her then!" She tapped her mouth in thought. "Kimmy?"

Kevin turned bright red.

"I *love* Kimberly. Good choice," Amanda said. "Now you just have to work up the courage."

"I really don't think I can," Kevin moaned.

"How about a game?" Tony suggested. "Something that all of us can play, so we won't be leaving you alone."

"Never Have I Ever?" Amanda suggested.

"Oh God, no!" Tony said with a chuckle. "We'd be drunk by the second round. Let's ask Glenn if he has anything prepared."

"Ah, so we'll all be naked by the second round," Amanda said with a nod. "That's much better."

"Jesus," muttered Kevin under his breath.

Tony twisted around, looking for his friend. He was deep in conversation with James, still leaning against the buffet. "What ho, Glenn!" he called.

"Nerd!" Glenn shouted back, but he made his way over. "What's up?"

"We were wondering if you had any games that all of us could play," Amanda asked.

"No swapping bodily fluids?" Glenn scoffed. "It's as if you don't know me."

Tony narrowed his eyes. "I'm not sure if that's a yes or a no. Could go either way in this case."

"Of course I have such a game. Although..." He trailed off, tapping his lips. "It's usually played with shots, but it's a little early in the day for that."

"Tell us the rules," James said. "Maybe we can come up with something as a replacement."

More people were paying attention to them now.

"Go around in a circle, one person being the focus. They roll a die. Whatever number it lands on, people have to guess whether they've done a thing." When Glenn realized people were confused, he rolled his eyes. "Okay, let's do an example. I'm the focus. I roll a dice, let's say it lands on two. Two people would tell me one assumption each that they've made about me, like, I don't know, I first had sex when I was fourteen, and my dick is bent to the left. I have to tell them how many they got right, one in this case, and they have to guess which one it is. If they guess right, I take a shot. If they guess wrong, play moves on to the next focus."

"Oh, that sounds like fun," Amanda said, clapping her hands.

"If you roll a one, you'll automatically lose," Tony said.

"Luck of the roll," Glenn replied with a shrug.

"What if, instead of a shot, you have to remove an article of clothing?" James suggested. "And then you have a chance to earn it back by getting someone else's assumptions correct?"

"See?" Amanda said in a loud aside to Kevin. "Naked by the second round."

Tony laughed. "I'm sure you mind greatly."

"Not at all," she chirped.

Kevin gulped. "I might have to get naked in front of everyone?"

"Don't worry," Tony said reassuringly. "It won't be just you."

"That's not very comforting," Kevin replied, eyeing Tony, and then James. "I'm not built like you," he added in a quieter tone.

Tony immediately turned serious. "If you don't feel comfortable taking off your clothes, you don't have to. We can come up with a different penalty for you and others like you."

Kevin blinked. "You would?"

"Absolutely," Amanda said. "Exhibitionism isn't for everyone. I'd be hesitant if my boys weren't here."

"No peer pressure involved," James added. "The point of the game is to get you to relax, not make you feel uncomfortable."

Kevin nodded slowly. "Okay."

"Don't worry. You won't go first," Amanda said, patting his shoulder. "You can think about it until then."

Glenn, who had been silent, piped up. "Lose an article of clothing or do a silly dance for ten seconds? Does that seem fair? And it applies across the board. Anyone can choose which option they want at any time. Although if you're already naked, you have to do the dance."

Amanda shoved him. "Or back out of the game," she pointed out.

"I suppose, if you want to be *boring*," Glenn replied dramatically.

"You just want to swing your dick around," Tony said with a chuckle. "We've all seen it before. Nothing to write home about."

"Just because I'm not hung like a horse doesn't mean I don't get the job done," Glenn replied with a sniff. "At least I don't have to worry about hurting the girl if I don't prep her enough."

"Prep her enough?" James held a hand over his heart. "Dude."

"What?" Glenn replied.

Tony shook his head. "If you have to ask, you're doing it wrong. Prep is one of the best parts."

Glenn glanced between the two guys before bowing to Amanda. "You must be the luckiest woman in the world."

"I absolutely am. You'd better start the game before I decide to drag these two off for a repeat of this morning," she replied.

By the time Glenn had managed to get everyone organized—they'd decided to head out to the heated patio because there was more space for everyone to sit in a circle—the stragglers had come downstairs for breakfast and joined them.

The large number of people meant that it took a while for the focus to come around to them. They shouted out assumptions about Glenn's college friends, but they didn't know them, so very few people lost any clothing.

Finally, it was Tony's turn, and he rolled a one.

"Damn," he sighed. "Hit me."

"I got one," Damien piped up from halfway around the circle. "You were fucking Amanda at fourteen."

"Zero right," Tony replied.

"Bullshit!" Damien shouted.

"No, he's right," Amanda said. "I didn't have sex with him when we were fourteen."

Damien and Ben put their heads together, but Tony rolled his eyes and ignored them.

"Since it's pretty obvious which assumption is right, I automatically lose an article of clothing, right?" Tony checked with Glenn.

"Or do a dance," Glenn reminded him.

"I don't mind," Tony said, stripping off his shirt.

"Me neither," Amanda purred, running her hand over his shoulders.

"Your turn, darlin'," Tony said, passing her the dice.

"Sure." She rolled a two. "Hit me with it."

"You've taken both guys at once!" shouted someone Tony didn't know from across the circle.

"You lost your virginity to James!" Ben shouted.

"One is correct," Amanda said, wiggling in her seat and smiling slightly.

After much back-and-forth between the high school crowd and the new people, the consensus was that she'd lost her virginity to James was the false assumption.

"Good job!" Amanda said happily, hauling her oversized t-shirt over her head and dropping it behind her. She was wearing a string bikini that barely covered her, the curve of her breasts making Tony's mouth water. "Here you go, James."

He rolled a three.

Ben immediately suggested that James and Tony had been fucking at fourteen.

Tony remembered the soccer tournament that had started that particular rumor. It was hard to keep the laughter hidden.

"Your cock is bigger than Tony's!"

Tony raised a skeptical eyebrow at that one. At least half the people at the party had seen them naked when everyone had been skinny dipping. But it was a friend of Glenn's that he'd never met before. *Only mildly true, but still true,* he thought.

"You're always on top!"

Not true, but James did give off 'Big Top' energy, Tony couldn't argue with that.

"One is correct," James said with a slight chuckle.

That provoked even more arguing than Amanda's, but eventually the correct assumption was decided upon, and James lost his shirt, much to Damien and Ben's shock.

Next was Kevin, but everyone guessed incorrectly for his assumption, so he didn't have to make a choice.

A few people later, Kevin's crush Kimberly had her turn, and she lost her shirt. "At least I learned not to wear a dress with no bra to your parties, Glenn," she said with a giggle. Her breasts were as covered as Amanda's, but the material strained to contain her.

"To everyone's loss," Glenn teased, making her blush.

A few more rounds, and nearly everyone was down to one article of clothing or less, fighting to earn the right to regain items. Even the people who had initially been reluctant to remove clothing had felt more comfortable after the first round.

"I feel like this game has outlived its usefulness, don't you think?" Tony asked, leaning over so his partners could hear him.

Amanda shook her head. "Kevin looks just as nervous as he did before we started. We can't just leave him."

"You're right," James said with a grin. "Want to increase the heat?"

"What do you mean?" she asked, squirming a little between them.

"I think we've been very good about keeping our hands to ourselves," Tony murmured. "Even though you took off your bikini top before your shorts and let everyone stare at your gorgeous breasts."

"I didn't want to get up," she protested weakly.

"And you like showing off," James added. "So let's show you off."

Amanda swallowed hard. "Like you promised you would last night?"

Tony groaned, pinching the bridge of his nose to stave off the images that reminder evoked. James had suggested that he would fuck her against a table in front of everybody this morning. But it was one thing to get naked during a game along with everyone else, and another entirely to start fucking. Not without the explicit consent of everyone present.

James's eyes flared with heat. "Perhaps. If that's what you want, sunshine."

"Fuck, Jamie," Tony ground out. "I'm getting obscene over here."

His partners stared at his red boxer briefs and smirked when his cock twitched under their attention.

"Not helping," he complained half-heartedly.

"Not trying to," James said. "Sunshine, make out with him while I go chat with Glenn."

A lapful of his girlfriend was hard to ignore. Half-naked and pressed against his erection, he was a goner.

Her lips connected with the corner of his mouth, slow and sweet, gauging his interest in the exhibitionism of the situation.

He was fucking interested.

Groaning, he wrapped his arms around her bare back, her long blonde hair tangling in his fingers. She met his fervor with her own, rolling her hips down and setting his nerves on fire.

The heat built between them, breath mingling as his hands trailed down to her barely clothed ass, helping keep her rhythm steady.

A gentle hand on his shoulder brought his attention back to their surroundings.

"Glenn is fine with changing up the game," James said. "How do you two feel about playing Sex Twister?"

Amanda broke the kiss, and Tony trailed his lips down her neck. "What are the rules?" she gasped.

"Pick a partner, and they'll be your mat. Instead of hands and feet, it's hands and mouth. The colors become body parts; breasts, mouth, and genitals. You in?" James grinned at them.

"Fuck yes," Tony moaned into her collarbone. "Extended foreplay? Absolutely."

James chuckled. "I thought you'd agree. I've already made the spinner." He raised his voice, "Everyone ready?"

With great difficulty, Tony pulled his attention away from Amanda to check on Kevin. Somehow James had managed to pair him up with Kimberly. The pair looked nervous but pleased with the arrangement.

"First spin," James said. "Right hand, breast."

Amanda whimpered when Tony tweaked her nipple, rocking her hips against him. "Oh God, that feels so good. This is going to be torture, isn't it?"

Tony chuckled. "The best kind of torture, I think."

"Left hand, genitals." James wasn't pulling any punches.

"Can I take this off?" Tony asked, flicking the ties at the side of her bikini.

Instead of answering, Amanda yanked at the knots, the scrap of fabric falling between them.

"Good enough for me," Tony said, unerringly rolling her clit between his thumb and finger.

She bucked in his lap. "Ohmigod Tony!" she gasped.

"Yeah, I got you, darlin'," he said encouragingly. "You're soaking wet. This is really getting you off, isn't it?"

Her fingernails dug into his shoulders. "No shit," she muttered.

"Right hand, mouth," James called out.

Amanda obediently dropped her jaw and Tony rested his fingers on her tongue. She closed her mouth and sucked.

The suction went straight to his cock.

A muffled cry of pleasure reached his ears, but since it wasn't Amanda's, he mentally brushed it aside.

"Mouth, genitals," James said.

"You're going to have to lie back," Tony said encouragingly.

There was a flurry of motion around them as everyone found better positions for the game. Tony wasted no time getting his mouth on her clit, the fingers of his left hand moving to press inside her. The flood of arousal that met them made his eyes roll back. She was going to feel so good around his cock after the game.

"Oh *fuck*, Tony!" Amanda moaned around his fingers, her hand flying to his hair to press his head harder against her body.

"Mouth, breast," James said.

"No!" Amanda shouted, making several people laugh.

The clenching around his fingers told him that she'd been close to coming. Adjusting his position, he latched onto her nipple, drawing the hard little bud into his mouth and treating it to the same tongue lashing that he'd given her clit. Meeting her eyes, he cocked an eyebrow in question.

"Please," she whimpered, giving another hard suck to his fingers.

He began to thrust harder, the wet squelch music to his ears. His thumb grazed her clit and she arched under him, heels digging into his calves as she exploded.

He didn't give her time to come down, adding a third finger and scissoring them.

Amanda flailed, one hand grabbing his wrist and the other the decking underneath them.

Kimberly, nearby, reached out to take her hand, and the girls gripped each other tightly.

"Right hand, breast," James said.

"*Fuck*, Tony!" Amanda shouted as soon as her mouth was free. "Yes, right there!"

Kimberly moaned in response.

James is a fucking genius, Tony thought, his mouth switching sides so his fingers could pluck at the wet nipple.

"Mouth, mouth," James said, and Tony enthusiastically joined their mouths again, welcoming Amanda's tongue in a dance along his. She was lax against him, her body pliant to his ministrations.

"Left hand, mouth," James said.

Amanda groaned her complaint, her orgasm dancing out of reach again.

Tony hummed as her tart flavor hit their tongues at the same time.

"Mouth, genitals," James coached.

Tony didn't need to be told twice, moving down her body to devour her juices. The only problem was that he didn't have his hands free to hold her hips down. She was thrusting against his face, grinding her clit against his nose.

"I think everyone's in a pretty good place now, so I'll let you continue on your own. Happy orgasms!" James said cheerfully.

"I've got condoms if you need them!" Glenn called out. "Just raise your hand and I'll bring them around. No pressure, of course."

James's shoulders nudged Tony as he settled beside him. "I'm parched."

"She's dripping," Tony said, leaning back slightly.

"Good job, cowboy." James pulled Tony into a searingly messy kiss, cleaning his chin and lips with his tongue.

By the end of it, Tony was panting as hard as Amanda.

"Fuck, guys. I need you inside me," she whined. "Can you, please?"

"How do you want us?" James asked, idly circling her clit with a finger.

"I don't know," she moaned. "Is there lube?"

"Good question." Tony reluctantly turned his attention to his surroundings. The couples were in various positions. Kevin was still eating Kimberly out, and she seemed to be enjoying herself immensely. He got Glenn's attention, and the man picked his way through limbs to get to him.

"What's up, other than your dick?" Glenn teased.

"Do you have lube?"

"Straight to the point. Of course I do. What am I, new?" Glenn dug through the wicker basket he had on his arm like an Easter Bunny. "Aha! Lube." He tossed Tony the packet. "Condoms?"

Tony tilted his head at Amanda.

"Oh God, James!" she whimpered. "Fuck, there, yes, *fuck*!"

"Just in case," Tony said, holding his hand out.

"Tony, no," she gasped, her hips writhing. "It's fine. Don't need one. Special occasion."

His eyebrows rose. "Okay, you're the boss. Thanks, man." He flapped the lube at him in acknowledgement.

"You're not stretched enough for that," James commented.

"I didn't know she wanted that," Tony replied.

"Then stretch me!" she ordered.

Tony chuckled. "As you wish, darlin'." He watched James scissor three fingers apart, her body stretching around him, and had to grip his cock to stave off his orgasm. Once the danger had passed, he bent his head over her clit to make her fly once more.

By the time she was ready to take them, most of the other couples had finished and were lazily making out or watching the others.

"You sure—" James began, but Amanda cut him off.

"Get inside me now!" she growled.

"You don't have to ask me twice," Tony said, finally shucking his briefs. The material had a wet spot at the head of his cock, and it had been chafing for the last— Well, he hadn't been paying attention to the time.

"You're under," James said, and Tony hurried to obey, sitting beside Amanda and liberally lubing up his cock.

Together, they manoeuvred her to straddle him, and once she had taken him, he laid down with her on his chest. He pumped his hips up into her a few times while watching James strip off his briefs. The man was sex on a stick.

"Pull up a bit, oh good girl," James purred as he slid in. "Does that feel good?"

Tony clenched his jaw tight, the space inside her suddenly feeling as close to heaven as he could imagine.

"Feels fucking fantastic," Amanda moaned. "Make me come, please."

"Again?" James teased, slowly pumping his hips. "You know who deserves to come? Tony. He's given you multiple orgasms today."

Amanda propped herself up slightly, just enough to look at Tony. "You're going to come first," she said.

"Most likely," he ground out. He was pinned between the hard decking and his two lovers.

There was no way he could thrust, so instead, he grabbed her hips and helped her rise and fall on top of him. Her breasts swayed from the slight movement, her nipples brushing his chest hair.

"What do you need?" James asked.

"Harder," Tony said.

Amanda nodded vehemently. "And fingers on my clit."

"I can do that," Tony said. He managed to get his hand between their bodies before James slammed his hips against her, and his vision whited out. He rubbed over her clit like an amateur, his entire focus directed to the smooth friction over his cock.

Two more hard thrusts, and he was gone. James was next, the warmth of his cum mixing with Tony's. He pulled his scattered brain together enough to hit the perfect rhythm on her clit, and Amanda joined them, her inner muscles squeezing them tighter together as she shouted her pleasure to the open air.

Breathing hard and sweating, James disentangled himself while Amanda collapsed her weight on Tony's chest.

"Daaaaaaaaaaamn," Glenn said, dragging the word out while he slow-clapped. "After that fire show, who's up for round two?"

Tony and James exchanged sheepish glances.

"Sorry, man," Tony said at last.

"Don't be fucking sorry!" Glenn exploded. "I nearly came in my pants!"

James laughed. "Mood."

"Happy Thanksgiving," Amanda said weakly, waving her hand. "Your present is live porn of your best friends. You're welcome."

Laughing, Glenn bowed theatrically. "I might beg for an encore."

"Give us a few," Tony said. "And maybe a damp cloth? Darlin', you're leaking onto me."

"Sorry." She didn't move or sound sorry in the slightest. "Kimmy, how's it going?"

He stretched his arms and then rested his head on his hands. From his prone position, he couldn't see the rest of the party, other than either side of him.

Kimberly was in a similar position to Amanda, lying on top of Kevin, who looked completely blissed out. "Amazing," she murmured. "I don't think I can move."

"Nice." Tony held out his fist to Kevin, who tapped it weakly. "Good game."

Part Two:

The Motorcycle

This takes place about 4 years after they start living together

"It sucks that Tony had to go out today," pouted Amanda, one hot Sunday afternoon in July. She lay naked in the middle of the bed, hair spread around her head like a halo.

"I can't imagine the heat," said a naked James from the doorway. He leaned against the frame, eyes half closed as he admired her. "And he'll be back by dinner. His errands shouldn't take too long."

Amanda ran her fingers lightly over her body, making eye contact with him. "Do you think it's as hot out there as it is in here?" she asked.

"No." James growled lowly. "Are you going to give me a show, or are you trying to entice me back to bed?"

"Neither," she purred. "It feels nice." Her fingers dipped in between her legs, rubbing over slightly sore muscles.

"I bet it does." He grinned. "Don't let my being here stop you."

"Actually, I have an idea." Amanda removed her fingers from her body and beckoned him closer. He crawled on top of her and pressed kisses up her body, leaving her breathless. "I want you to sit on the edge of the bed and put on this blindfold." From behind her back, she produced a thick black scarf. "I want you to listen to me make myself come, but you can't do anything to help, or watch."

One corner of his mouth ticked up in a smirk. "Sounds torturous," he murmured. "What do I get out of it?"

"What do you want?" she asked, biting down on his earlobe.

"I'll have to think about that," he hummed. "Are you up for anything?"

"I will do anything for you," Amanda purred. "Now go sit over there."

James grinned. "Yes, mistress." He kissed her one more time before pushing off her and over to the edge of the bed. He took the scarf and tied it over his eyes once he sat down. "Am I allowed to touch myself?"

"Yes, but you aren't allowed to orgasm," ordered Amanda.

She reached into her drawer for her fingertip vibrator and turned it on. Running it lightly over her clit, she moaned loudly, "Ooh, James, this feels so good."

James squirmed in his seat.

With her other hand, she slipped two fingers inside herself. A flood of wetness met them and she groaned, "You make me so wet, James."

She pumped her fingers a couple times before sliding a third, and fourth. "I am so wet, I could probably fit my whole fist inside myself," she teased, gasping. "Oh God…"

James groaned and let his hand grasp his cock. "Fuck, that's a visual."

Her vibrator danced over her clit as she pumped her hand slickly into herself. "Can you hear how wet I am?" she panted. "James, I'm going to come!"

"Come, baby. I want to hear you come," breathed James.

Amanda pressed down hard with her vibrator and screamed with pleasure, her release rocking through her body. She clenched around her fingers, her muscles shaking with the intensity of her orgasm.

"That sounded so amazing," James growled. He moved his hands to take off the blindfold, and Amanda stopped him.

"I'm not done yet," she said shakily.

"Sunshine, you're killing me here," he groaned.

"Be patient," she purred. She slid off the bed and circled around to him.

"Damn," murmured James. He reached out for her, grabbing her hips. "Are you going to fuck me?"

"Yes." Amanda straddled his lap and led his cock to her dripping pussy. He slid inside her easily, right to the hilt. "You bet I am," she groaned. She circled her hips on top of him, enjoying the feeling of complete control. "Suck on my nipple," she gasped. Unerringly, James bent his head to her breast and latched on, lapping at her nipple with his tongue.

She gasped and closed her eyes. When she opened them, Tony was standing in the doorway, watching them with a grin. He put his finger to his lips when he noticed her looking at him. Quietly, he began to remove his clothes, and gestured from himself to James. Amanda nodded, understanding what Tony was suggesting.

"James, I want you on top of me," she panted.

Without missing a beat, James stood up, turned, and dropped her gently on the bed. She wrapped her legs around his waist, clinging to his body, and he lifted her higher up the bed. He rolled his hips into hers and dropped a kiss onto her collarbone. "Aren't you impressed?" he drawled.

"Very," gasped Amanda. "Ooh, James, this feels good."

"Let me make it feel fucking fantastic," growled Tony, startling James. Tony rubbed the lube he had grabbed from beside the condoms onto James' ass before climbing onto the bed behind him. "When I thrust in, you thrust in," he murmured to them, and then pushed his way inside James.

"Holy fuck," panted James.

The three of them moved their hips in sync with each other, struggling to retain control. The added pressure of Tony's thrusts forced James's cock into Amanda deeper than ever.

"Oh my God," she cried out. "I'm going to come!"

"Fuck, Tony," groaned James. "So am I."

"Yes," hissed Tony. "Come with me! Now!" He gave one last brutal thrust into James, spilling inside the condom that sheathed his cock.

James and Amanda followed him over the edge, panting with the force of their release.

They collapsed on the bed in a heap. James removed the blindfold. "I rather enjoy sensory deprivation," he said thoughtfully. "Occasionally." He winked.

"Did you guys do anything besides have sex since I left?" Tony teased after catching his breath.

"Yes," replied Amanda defensively.

"We went for a nice long run this morning," added James.

"Uh huh." Tony chuckled. "I have something to show you, but you gotta put on some clothes."

They untangled themselves and got dressed. Tony's eyes gleamed with approval when he saw that Amanda had put on a short black skirt and a red halter. "That looks amazing on you, love," he told her. "That outfit is perfect!" He handed her a pair of ankle boots. "These will match nicely." He winked, and picked up his black leather jacket on the way out the door.

Parked against the curb, glittering in the sun, was a sleek red and black motorcycle. Tony threw the coat over the engine. "What do you think?" he asked his friends proudly.

"Oh, Tony!" Amanda breathed. "That is the sexiest thing I have ever seen."

"I fell in love with it the moment I saw it." Tony beamed. "It's a Kawasaki Ninja."

"Have you named it yet?" asked James, admiring the bike. "It's beautiful."

"I was thinking of 'Kitten,' because she purrs so sweetly." Tony grinned. "I'm going to take both of you for a ride. But first, we need to go get your gear."

"Can I sit on it before we go back inside?" asked Amanda wistfully. "Just to see how it feels?"

"Of course!" Tony helped her to mount and straddle the bike, and then stepped back, taking his coat with him. "Damn," he whistled. "You should model bikes for a living."

Amanda tossed her hair over her shoulder and leaned forwards to grip the handles. "Even off, I can feel the power between my legs," she purred. Letting go of the handles, she placed her hands behind her on the passenger seat and arched backwards, thrusting her breasts into the air.

"If you keep doing poses like that," said James in a strangled voice, "We won't be going anywhere but back into the house."

She giggled, lying all the way back on the bike, her hair falling over the sides. "Posing like what?" she teased.

Tony groaned and picked her off the seat, setting her down on the ground. "You know exactly what you're doing to us," he told her, trying to sound stern. "I want to take you for a ride."

"I want you to take me for a ride, too," she murmured in his ear.

Tony's hands tightened reflexively on her waist. "Oh, don't you worry," he growled. "But I can't take you anywhere until you're properly dressed." He let go of her reluctantly and grabbed his silver helmet from the lock at the back of the bike. "Go get your gear from the back."

They had bought the necessary protective gear a few days before, but hadn't been sure of when Tony would be able to get the motorcycle itself. The dealership had told him it wouldn't be until sometime next week.

"I'll just take you once around the block," said Tony to James.

"Yeah you will." James waggled his eyebrows.

Amanda giggled.

Tony tried to ignore them, but gave up with a grin. "When we turn, hold on to me and lean the way I do. Don't be scared and lean the other way, everything will be fine. Trust me. Grip my hips with your knees to keep yourself from sliding around."

He helped James put on his helmet before putting on his own. Tony slipped on his jacket and zipped up, and then swung a leg over the bike and settled into place. He started up the motor, grinned at the growling purr, and brought the kickstand up. "Ready?" he asked James.

James paused to appreciate the view of Tony straddling the bike. "I was born ready!"

"Then come on up behind me." James settled into place on the passenger seat behind him, and held Tony's waist tightly. "Don't move around too much," Tony said over his shoulder. "Kitten is a light and fast bike, so every movement will impact our balance on this baby."

"Gotcha," replied James.

Tony revved the motor a few times and felt the vibrations course through them. He snicked it into gear, they waved to Amanda, and then pulled away smoothly and quickly down the street.

Amanda sat on the bottom step, her black helmet, chaps, and jacket next to her. Starting a French braid in her hair, she absent-mindedly watched a squirrel run down the tree shading her. It scampered across the sidewalk to a planter at the front of the house, leapt up onto it, and then dug beside a small cedar. "Stop that," she told it. The squirrel ignored her. She sighed and finished the plait in her hair, tying it off with an elastic that she was wearing around her wrist. She then slipped on her chaps, tightly securing the belt at her waist.

A low roar made her ears prick up, a sound like thunder coming closer, and the motorcycle came into view. When they pulled up in front of her, she could tell from their body language that the ride had gone well. She got up and walked towards the bike, the unzipped chaps swinging between her legs. A practiced flip of the kill switch silenced the bike, and James swung himself off the back of the bike.

"That was amazing," said James, the broad grin on his face visible the instant he took off his helmet. "I definitely want to go for a longer ride next time!"

"We'll make a date of it," replied Tony, his voice muffled by his helmet. He flipped up the visor. "One night this week."

James grinned his approval, and then grabbed Amanda to him one-armed. "Don't you look fucking fantastic in those?" He ran his hand over her skirt, the open back of the chaps granting him easy access. "Promise of things to come," he growled, kissing her passionately.

"Wow," Amanda panted when he released her. "If one block on this thing makes you this horny, how will a longer ride affect you?"

He smacked her ass, pulling her even closer to grind their pelvises together. "You'll have to tell me," he groaned.

Tony beckoned to Amanda. "Where do you want to go, my love?"

"I have no preference."

"You need to do up your chaps," Tony pointed out.

"Hold my helmet and jacket for me?" she asked as she handed them over to him. Then she turned away and bent over, fastening the zipper at the top of her left thigh, and slowly pulled it down to her ankle. She heard a smothered groan when she reached the bottom of the pant leg. "See anything you like?" she asked innocently. She paused before clicking the three snaps at the bottom, giving him a better view before standing upright. She repeated the process on the right leg.

"I see a whole lot of what I like." Tony smirked. "Including one of my favourite pairs of your underwear."

"You sneaked a peek?" Amanda acted shocked.

"How could I not?" he replied lowly, pulling her closer by her belt. "Let's get the rest of your gear on before I change my mind about what sort of a ride you're going to take."

She shivered with anticipation, taking back her helmet and putting it on with Tony's help. She shrugged into her black leather jacket while Tony admired how it settled against her figure. It covered her red halter, which was mildly disappointing, but it fit snugly, highlighting her curves. Her black chaps opened at the front and back, allowing for a sliver of skin to peek out from under her skirt. Her short black boots had a low heel on them, which gave her legs a killer shape.

Bringing the bike upright, Tony winked at her through the narrow slit in his helmet visor.

She put one foot on the back peg, and holding onto Tony's shoulders, swung her leg over the back of the bike, settling onto the seat as James had done. Snuggling up to Tony's back, she kept her hands carefully on his waist.

"Where to?" he asked again.

"Somewhere private?" she suggested wickedly. "I want to really try out this bike."

Tony clenched his hands in his lap. "Fuck, you can't give me that sort of visual right before I start her up! I need to concentrate."

"Sorry," Amanda replied contritely. "Hairy men in speedos."

"What?" Tony laughed.

"Spiders, airport security, ripped up sneakers," suggested Amanda. "I'm trying to think of the un-sexiest things possible."

Still chuckling, Tony started up the bike again. This time it was Amanda who was treated to the vibrations of the motor. She gasped as she felt them through the seat, sending shocks straight to her clit.

"Hang on," he told her as he slipped the bike into gear and fed it some throttle. Amanda gulped, clutching him tightly, and they took off down the street.

Amanda squeaked and hung on tighter, closing her eyes. When nothing terrible happened after a few moments, she opened her eyes again. Tony leaned into a turn, and she followed his movements, melding to his body. She could feel his thigh muscles clenching to keep their balance. She got used to the motion of the bike as he entered the highway, and relaxed a fraction. This was all about trust, and she trusted him completely.

As they sped along the road, she realized they were heading west, away from Boston's downtown core. The wind tugged at them, and a feeling of exultation bubbled up in her.

This is incredible, she thought giddily. *I could get addicted to this feeling of freedom. I feel high on life.*

Tony wound their way through the outskirts of town, heading towards a stretch of nowhere just off the highway. Once they got there, Tony turned off the bike, kicked the stand down, and put his helmet delicately over the mirror.

"I can't get mine off," grumbled Amanda, fiddling with the strap under her chin.

He grabbed her leg, wrapped it over his, and swung her around onto his lap. With a smooth motion, he unclipped, removed, and placed her helmet over the other mirror. Their lips were instantly locked together as they fought to get their jackets off. Those became a pile on the ground, and Tony's palms found her breasts. She gasped, grinding her body on top of his.

He grabbed her ass, hands kneading the smooth flesh. "How are you feeling? I know that seat can be a little uncomfortable," he mumbled into her mouth.

"Just fine, oh God, Tony," she moaned. She was tucked tightly between the gas tank and his body, and she loved feeling constricted.

"Fuck, I need to feel you," he groaned into her mouth, and then his fingers were inside her underwear, thrusting them to the side, sliding slickly inside her.

"God, Tony," Amanda panted. She squeezed her internal muscles around his fingers. "I want you. That ride was foreplay."

"I'm not sure you're ready for me," he teased. He withdrew his fingers and fumbled at his belt.

Amanda undid the buttons down the front of his jeans, grateful for the lack of zipper, and pulled his cock out. "What, no underwear today?" she teased him back, stroking him slowly.

"I had a sneaking suspicion that something like this might happen, and I didn't want any further hindrance," he said, smirking. He lifted her body over his. She sank onto him easily, taking him deep inside of her.

She grasped his shoulders, using her upper body strength to drag herself along him. Tony helped her move, lifting her up by her perfect ass. Their mouths found each other again, tongues dancing, as she rocked against him. She broke away from his mouth to kiss and nip along his jawline up to his ear.

"I take it you like the bike," he growled.

"Feeling you controlling all that power as you guided her here was unbelievably sexy," she purred into his ear before biting on the lobe.

Tony groaned at the feeling. "If you keep doing things like that, I will not be held responsible for my actions."

She ground her hips down on him hard, and clenched her muscles around him. "You know I like it when you get rough," she moaned.

"Oh fuck, darlin'," Tony growled. Without removing her from his cock, he got off the bike, turned around, and straddled it again, facing the opposite direction. He laid her down over the seats. "Hold on tightly," he ordered, grabbing her hips. She reached over her head, grabbing the back of the passenger seat, and, muscles flexing, he slammed her onto his cock. Her screams of pleasure rang through the woods around them as he set a brutal pace, forcing his body into hers again and again.

"Tony!" she cried out. "Fuck, Tony, I –"

She broke off her words with a shout.

"Come for me, Amanda," he growled. "Let the world hear you come!"

"Yes! Tony, oh God, yes!" She fell apart in his arms, her thighs tightening around his hips and forcing him to stop moving. Her internal muscles milked his release from him, squeezing his cock with blinding force.

"Holy fuck," he ground out, once he could speak.

"I think I'm in love with this bike," said Amanda dreamily. "That was fucking amazing."

"Hey, I had a little part in this," chuckled Tony.

"Yes, you did." Amanda sat up, his cock shifting inside her at her movements. She gripped his t-shirt and pulled his mouth down to hers.

He wrapped one arm around her waist, the other around her shoulders, pulling her body tighter to his as their lips moved in rhythm.

He felt his cock twitch inside her, and broke the kiss, panting. "I don't think I can go again so soon, despite evidence to the contrary," he groaned.

"I could," teased Amanda. "I'm insatiable."

Tony groaned. "Don't I know it!" He slapped her ass lightly. "Time to go home, I think."

Amanda ran her fingers over the tattoos on his arm. "I like that. Get James in on this action."

"Sounds like a plan."

"And you can recover a bit on the way home."

"Brat."

She stuck her tongue out at him playfully.

Part Three:

Baby, I Love You

This takes place 6 years after the end of I Knew I Loved You

"I'm ovulating!" read Amanda's text. Tony had just arrived at work, but it almost had him racing home.

The only thing that kept him in his seat was the fact that she was at work too.

He resisted texting James, who was teaching until lunch.

Instead, Tony replied, "How am I going to survive until the end of day?"

Her response came in quickly. "Need some incentive?"

Tony groaned, rubbing his face with one hand. "I'm going to regret this either way," he muttered, sending an affirmative.

A picture came through, taken in their bathroom mirror, of Amanda in a dark green bra and panty set. The words, "Glad I thought ahead then!" and a winky face followed.

"Fuuuuuuuuuck me," Tony mumbled, eyes wide. He zoomed in on the picture and nearly swallowed his tongue when he realized that the material was practically sheer.

"Morning, Tony," chirped his coworker, squeezing past his desk to get to her own.

He dropped his phone with a clatter as she made herself comfortable in their two-person cubicle.

"Hey, Mallory," he squeaked.

She rolled her eyes. "Which one was it this time?"

"What?"

"Which spouse texted you a message that put that goofy smile on your face?"

"Oh." He hadn't been aware he was broadcasting. "Amanda."

Mallory nodded. "Big date?"

"Uh huh. Yup." Tony quickly checked that he'd managed to hit the power button to turn off his screen. "The biggest."

"Right." She narrowed her eyes at him. "Did you know that you're a terrible liar?"

"Only if you know me," he muttered.

She reached over to pat his shoulder. "We've been coworkers for how many years now? I like to think I know you pretty well." Tony's ears turned pink and Mallory laughed. "Oh. *That* kind of text."

"Shut up."

"No! I think it's sweet that you're still blushing from a sext from your wife after what, five years of marriage?"

"Six this Christmas," he said, his gaze finding the framed picture of the three of them on their wedding day on his desk. "And it wasn't a sext."

"Uh huh." Mallory shot him a skeptical look. "Anything that gets you all blushy like an adolescent with his first crush is bound to be a sext. But," she sighed dramatically. "I'm willing to believe you if you show me." She stretched out her hand and gestured for his phone.

"Nope. Not falling for that," Tony said, tucking his phone in his front pocket and nudging his mouse to wake up his computer.

"It's funny that you're embarrassed about sexting your wife," Mallory said, swivelling her chair to face her own desk.

"I'm not. And she sent a picture."

Mallory whistled low. "At this hour? She tryna kill ya?"

Tony snorted. "Right?" He hit print on the files he'd set up the day before. "Two families today."

"Tough ones?"

"Potentially." Tony sighed and got to his feet, pulling on his leather jacket. "See you at lunch."

"You're not going to sneak into your wife's office?"

Tony paused in folding the papers he'd just printed. "That hadn't occurred to me," he admitted sheepishly.

"Dude, you're losing your edge." Mallory shook her head. "Go sweep her off her feet!"

"Yeah, I think I might do that." He stuffed the papers in an inside pocket of his coat and zipped up. "See you at the end of day then."

"I gotta question." Mallory leaned back in her chair so far he worried it might topple backwards.

"Shoot."

"Do you dress like a fifties greaser because you think it makes you look tough and the kids will relate to you better, or is this just your style?"

Tony grabbed his motorcycle helmet from the top of the filing cabinet and rolled his eyes. "Do you dress like a seventies flower child for the same reason?"

"Touché."

He nodded, rapped his knuckles on her desk in farewell, and strode out of the office to his red Ninja.

To be perfectly honest, he loved his style, which was *not* fifties greaser but more motorcycle punk, *and* the kids he went to see usually did trust him faster when he pulled up in front of their house with a roar.

He called it *the cool factor* in his mind, not that he would ever tell anyone at work that.

The powerful engine between his thighs, he pulled out into the morning Bostonian traffic, heading for his first stop of the day.

The house was in a suburb, perfectly trimmed grass and award-winning flowerbeds in front of each house. There was no indication that children lived there based on the front yards, though there was an elementary school within walking distance.

He pulled up in front of a beige house that was a cookie-cutter version of all the others and pulled out his phone to check the address.

The last text from Amanda greeted him, and he smiled before swiping away from it to his appointments app. The address matched, so he got off the bike, his long legs eating up the driveway to the front door.

He shook his hair out while he waited for the door to be answered, his helmet tucked under his arm. The worst part about having a motorcycle in summer was at the end of the ride: body all sweated up under a leather jacket and helmet and nowhere to store them.

The door opened to reveal a woman with a toddler on her hip. "Yes? Can I help you?" she asked, confused.

"Hello, Mrs. Vandermere. My name is Tony Carlson, and I'm with the DCF. We spoke on the phone about Damien?"

Her eyes widened, and she gave him a once-over. "Of course. You aren't exactly what we were expecting."

"I never am," Tony replied cheerfully. "Is Damien home?"

"He will be soon. My husband took him to the skatepark nearby. He knows to be back by ten."

"And I'm a little early. Sorry. Traffic wasn't too bad on my bike."

Her eyes dropped to his helmet again before widening in horror. "Oh, and here I am, keeping you out in the heat! Please, come in! Do you want some water?"

"That would be fantastic," Tony replied, following her into the house. "I never think about water when I'm setting out. It's always 'keys, wallet, phone,' and nothing else comes to mind."

Mrs. Vandermere laughed nervously. "I can see how it would be difficult to fit a water bottle on a motorcycle. Unless it comes with cup holders?"

"Those were extra," he teased, stepping out of his boots.

"Oh."

"I'm joking."

"Oh! Sorry, I don't know much about them." The woman flushed, waving her free hand in the air.

"That's okay." Tony glanced around the living room of the house while she escaped to the kitchen to get him a glass, noting the baby toys scattered around the room. "Damien's been with you for a month now? How's he settling in?" he asked when she returned.

"Oh, I don't know." She put the baby down on the ground, who immediately crawled over to a set of sorting blocks. "He's very quiet. He hardly ever addresses us. I told him he could call me 'Mom' if he felt comfortable, but he hasn't."

"That's completely normal," Tony reassured her. He sat on the ground with the baby and handed over a block. "What does he like to do, beyond skateboarding?"

"He reads a lot. We go to the library for storytime with Bridget, and he's allowed to stay on his own outside the baby room. Is that okay?" She wrung her hands nervously. "We don't want to hover, give him some freedom."

"If he hasn't abused the privilege, you're doing the right thing. What about friends? Does he have social media? Is he still in contact with anyone from a previous fostering?"

"He doesn't have social media. We gave him a basic phone so he could contact us if he goes to the park on his own, but it doesn't have data. I hope he's not in contact with anyone we don't know." She bit her lip anxiously. "What do we do if he is?"

"One step at a time. Have you suggested pre-teen library book clubs, since he's already comfortable there?"

"They have those?"

"If they don't yet, they will if you ask. Librarians *love* doing stuff for kids."

"I feel like I should be making a list," she murmured.

"Feel free." Tony handed a cylinder to the baby and watched her try to put it in the triangle's slot with amusement.

The front door slammed open. "Mom! There's a *motorcycle* outside our house!" shouted a voice.

Tony's gaze snapped to Mrs. Vandermere to see her reaction. Her eyes filled with tears and her lip wobbled.

"Did you see it?" The boy who must be Damien burst into the room, skidding to a halt when he saw Tony sitting on the floor.

"Sorry for dropping by unannounced," Tony said. "I always hated it when social workers did that to me."

Damien's eyes widened. "You were like me?"

Tony smiled crookedly. "Always will be. Circumstances change, but our experiences shape who we are. I'll always be a foster kid."

"Bet I've had it worse," Damien scoffed.

"Wanna talk about it?" Tony asked gently.

Damien opened and closed his mouth a few times.

Tony took pity on him. "Do you want to see my motorcycle?"

"Can I ride it?"

"No."

Damien pouted for all of a second. "Okay."

"We'll be out front," Tony said, getting to his feet.

"Okay." Mrs. Vandermere's voice still sounded watery.

He shot her what he hoped she interpreted as an understanding glance and followed the boy outside.

Mr. Vandermere was puttering around in the garage, pulling out the lawn mower even though the grass looked the same height as everyone else's.

Shaking his head, he focused on the kid, who was walking around the motorcycle. Tony shrugged out of his leather jacket and draped it over the handlebars next to his helmet.

Damien stared at his full-sleeve tattoos in awe, the only thing that could have drawn his attention away from the bike. "You're not like the others."

"Hell no," Tony drawled, delighting the kid with his language. "I'm the punk they call in when they need someone cool."

"Yeah," Damien said, looking from him to the bike.

"That was a joke," Tony said, shaking his head with a chuckle.

Damien raised an eyebrow skeptically. "Sure."

Tony explained the different parts of the motorcycle and showed him how to start it up. "It's a lot like a manual transmission in a car. If you ever want to ride, you'll need to learn stick."

"I don't think they—" he gestured at the house, "—have that kind of car."

"Driver's ed instructors have their own cars. You could request a manual. But to be perfectly honest, it's a lot easier to learn automatic. You're already dealing with a ton of new info. Why add more? You can learn stick later." Tony sat on the grass and stretched his legs out. "So. You think you've had it worse than I did?"

Damien glanced up at him from the other side of the bike. "One house, I was their servant. Cleaning floors, washing dishes, doing laundry, you name it."

Tony nodded. "Modern-day Cinderella. Classic. Beatings if you messed up?"

"Bed without food."

"Right. Where'd you hoard it in your room?"

Damien smirked. "A hollowed-out Bible."

"Clever. I had a loose floorboard in the closet. Made friends with the rats."

"You really were like me." Damien circled around the bike to sit beside Tony.

"I never lie," Tony said seriously. "And that's a pretty horrible thing to lie about."

"I guess." The boy started pulling grass out between his legs one at a time.

Tony frowned, mentally reading over the kid's file in his mind. Something wasn't adding up. "I did learn some skills," he said. "Lock picking, for one."

"Really?" Damien looked excited. "Cool."

"Reading people was another."

The boy cocked his head. "What do you mean?"

"I can tell what kind of person I'm talking to within minutes of meeting them. First impressions are everything."

"What kind of person am I?"

"Kids are harder, but I'll give it a shot." Tony swiveled to face Damien, crossing his legs, and studied the boy's face. "You've been hurt by adults in the past, both broken promises and physically." Tony rubbed his chin. "You tried the tough act on the last house, acting out and being the most difficult you could be because then they'd see you at your worst and get rid of you. Then you could say, 'See? Nobody wants me.' You're afraid to trust again, but you're trying with this family... because of the baby?"

Damien nodded, looking taken aback. "She's pretty cute."

"She is." Tony leaned his elbows on his knees. "What do you think will happen when you slip up?"

"I won't." The boy clenched his jaw so hard it creaked.

"You will," Tony said gently. "Everyone has bad days. Give yourself grace."

"I... I don't know!" Damien looked panicked.

"What can you do to prepare yourself for the eventuality?"

"Hide food in my room?"

Tony chuckled. "Should have guessed you'd say that. No, don't do that. It attracts bugs, and this place isn't like your others."

"No kidding," Damien muttered.

"Two of the smartest people I know gave me really good advice when I was your age: it's better to come clean to your adults on your own rather than have them pry it out of you. They probably know the whole story already, and things will be easier for you if you tell your side of things before they've fully made up their minds on what punishment you might get."

"But what if they don't know, or don't care? Then me telling them that I got detention would just get me in trouble."

"Remember that skill I told you I was good at?"

"Lock picking?"

"The other one," Tony said with a chuckle. "Reading people. You're a smart kid. What do you think these adults are like? Do they care? Do you think they're invested in your life?"

"Yeeeess?"

"You don't sound sure."

"I'm not."

"Okay." Tony shrugged.

Damien blinked. "Okay?"

"Yup."

"The other social workers wouldn't say that."

"I told you, I'm the cool one." Tony grinned.

"If you really were cool, you wouldn't have to say it."

"Exactly." Tony nodded. "In all seriousness though, I can't force you to trust your adults. That's between you and them. How do you want to handle the rest of your life? Trusting people or being suspicious of them? You don't have to answer that. Think about it. New subject. Skateboarding! How's learning going?"

Damien looked confused. "I fall a lot."

"Of course you do. You've got protective gear though, right? I don't see scraped knees, so I assume so."

"Yeah. And a helmet."

"Still hurts, though, I bet. What do you do when you fall? Get back up?"

"Well, yeah. I'd get run over by someone else if I lie there."

"True enough. And you try again? How many times?"

"Until I'm exhausted. I'll get it eventually."

"Great attitude." Tony smiled a little and raised an eyebrow.

"What?"

"Can you apply your skateboarding experiences to any other aspects of your life?"

Understanding dawned across Damien's face like a sunrise. His jaw dropped. "How'd you do that?"

"Do what?" Tony pulled out a thick blade of grass and placed it between his thumbs, making a whistle. He blew hard, making a sharp sound. "We're just talking." He tightened his lips and blew again, higher this time. "Have you made any friends here?"

"The kids here are super stuck-up."

"Are you sure? Have you talked to them?"

"Well, no."

"How do you know they are? Maybe they're shy."

"Maybe," Damien mumbled.

Tony adjusted the blade of grass between his thumbs and blew again.

"Why are you doing that?"

"It's fun." Tony shrugged. "Don't you do things for fun?"

"I guess so."

"Like what?"

"Reading, listening to music, running. I don't know."

"All very solitary activities," Tony remarked.

"Obviously."

"Have you considered soccer?"

"I don't have the gear."

"School soccer and pick-up games don't require gear."

"I'll think about it."

Tony blew on the blade of grass, making it sound like a wet fart. Damien bit his lip to hide a smile. "Well, I think that's done," Tony said as if in surprise. "Did you want to head in now?"

"Sure." Damien shrugged. He hesitated, not getting up. "Did I..."

When he didn't continue the thought, Tony nodded. "Did you pass?"

Damien nodded, surreptitiously wiping his eyes.

"Did I make you feel like you were being tested?"

"No."

"Phew!" Tony said exaggeratedly, wiping his brow. "Good because I wasn't."

"You know what I mean." Damien scowled at his knees.

"You know I do." Tony waited until he had the boy's attention. "Do you feel unsafe here?"

"No!"

"Do you want to leave?"

"No."

"Great." Tony slapped his knees and got to his feet.

Damien stayed seated. "How do you do it?"

"Do what?"

"Become like you."

Tony snorted. "I'm not sure you're ready to hear the answer."

Damien scowled at him. "I'm not a baby."

"No, you're definitely not." Tony squatted down. "I don't want to preach. That's not what I'm here for."

"Church?" Damien made a face.

"No," Tony laughed. "I mean, that might help you. There are some great youth groups in churches. But you've made it clear that you're in a different place than I was when my life got turned around. I don't want you to feel like you have to follow my path just because it worked for me."

"Can't you tell me anyway?"

"When I moved to Massachusetts, I became friends with the two best people in the world. They are the reason I am the way I am today."

"Friends?" Damien groaned.

"See? I told you you wouldn't want to hear it." Tony ran a hand through his hair and grimaced at the sweat. "Friends are people who want stuff from you, right?"

"Right."

Tony shook his head. "Don't hang around people like that. Find the ones who like you for who you are, who make you want to be a better person for them."

"I see what you mean about preaching."

"I know, right?" Tony laughed. "But it's the truth. That's what worked for me. You'll find your way." He stood up again with an exaggerated groan. "I'm getting too old for this."

"What are you, fifty?"

Tony's jaw dropped. "Excuse you, I'm only thirty!"

"Old man."

"And damn proud of it." Tony nodded at Damien's wide eyes. "Don't say that word. But I am. When I was nine, I didn't think I'd live past fifteen."

"Bad family?"

"The worst, and that's saying something."

"What happened?"

Tony hesitated. He didn't often share his own story in detail, but there were exceptions. Damien reminded him so much of himself. "They were using us kids as drug mules across the border, and we got caught. I got put in a holding cell with the others. Then my social worker came to get me. Said he was putting me in a crappy orphanage, but they were the only ones willing to take me."

"Is that where you met your friends?"

"No." Tony bit back the expletive and took a deep breath. "The library was my refuge. I would go there every minute I could. There was a librarian who would suggest books. I never brought them home, though. I didn't want them stolen or destroyed. Eventually, we started talking. I had no idea that she knew I was an orphan; that she and her husband were going through the courts to get adoption papers set up. Not until she sat me down one day and asked if she could come visit me at my home to formally start an adoption. I'm not going to bore you with the details. It was not a smooth transition, but they never gave up on me, and finally came to the decision to get me out of Texas. We moved to Massachusetts, I met my best friends, and here I am."

"All because you went to the library?"

"I might be biased but the library is awesome, and so are people who read."

"Yeah." Damien stood up. "Thanks."

"Anytime. I mean that. Your adults have my number." Tony frowned. "Or will. I don't think I've given it yet. Do you feel comfortable asking them for it if you need it?"

Damien bit his lip as he thought.

"I usually suggest that the adults put it on the fridge or somewhere accessible," Tony said.

"Yeah, that works."

"It's my work number, and it's not on twenty-four-seven. If you have an emergency, the main number for the DCF is there. They have my personal info and can get a hold of me if you don't want to talk to anyone else. Does that work for you?"

"I guess."

"Do you expect an emergency?"

"No."

"Great. Let's go. I have a few more suggestions for your adults."

He gave Mrs. Vandermere a list of resources, including places for pre-teens to meet like Big Brothers Big Sisters and free programs run through the library. Damien perked up when he'd suggested the drop-in sports at the community center nearby.

"Imma head out. If you think of anything, gimme a call."

"Thank you," Mrs. Vandermere said.

"Not a problem. This is my favorite kind of visit." He looked down at Damien. "Anytime. Get it?"

"Got it."

"Good."

Mentally mapping out his route as he left the subdivision, Tony made his way through the busy streets to Amanda's building downtown. There was a florist two blocks down, which was his first stop. Then he headed into the multi-story building, signing in with security before they let him on the elevator.

Amanda's work rented space on the eighth floor, so the trip was relatively short. The massive double doors had been intimidating the first time he'd visited, but now he breezed through them.

"Mornin', Caitlyn," he greeted the young woman at the front desk. "Amanda in her office?"

She blushed and clicked on her computer. "She should be."

"Thanks." He threaded his way through the floor, greeting the people he knew, but single-mindedly heading for the corner office with the open door.

His wife was hunched over her computer, fiddling with the end of her ponytail with her free hand. She looked gorgeous. He adjusted his grip on his helmet and knocked on the door jamb.

Amanda lit up when she saw him and beamed even further when he handed her the two rosebuds. "What's the occasion?"

"Do I need an occasion to bring my wife flowers?"

"Of course not." She kissed his lips lightly. "But it feels like there's a message here."

Tony smiled. "The promise of beauty unfurling. Not knowing what the roses will look like until they bloom. I can't imagine what message rosebuds might mean."

Amanda flushed, wiggling a little. "You liked my text then?"

"Darlin', I can't stop thinking about it." He pressed her against the open door with his body, cupped her head in his free hand, and claimed her mouth with long, hot kisses that had her melting against him. "See you tonight, love," he whispered against her lips, and then he left, heart thudding at the abrupt end to the kiss. He was grateful for the extra coverage his helmet provided, or else her entire office would be able to see how hard he was.

The elevator ride to the lobby helped him calm down, and by the time he was astride his motorcycle again, he was focused on getting back to the office for lunch before a difficult afternoon.

By the end of the day, Tony was on edge. He'd been right about the second family visit being a difficult one. It was always hard when it was obvious that the adults were only in foster care for the stipend, but they weren't technically doing anything illegal.

He locked up his bike in their backyard, covering it with its tarp before heading up the back stairs to the kitchen.

James was stirring a sauce at the stove, the fan going full force.

"How was your day?" James asked while Tony bent to pick up his boots.

"Long. All I could think about was getting home," he admitted. He joined their lips for a moment, needing the familiar comfort.

"Yeah, that text this morning distracted me entirely. It took an hour for me to be able to focus on my class again. I made so many mistakes, the kids started to wonder if I needed a nap."

Tony chuckled. "Did she send you the lingerie photo too?"

"No." James's eyebrows rose in surprise.

"Here." Tony fished his phone out of his pocket. "She probably didn't want the kids to see it by accident."

James whistled when he saw the picture. "Good call on her part. Damn."

"She's not home yet, right?"

"No. What did you have in mind?"

"Do we still have those faux rose petals?"

"Have I told you I love you lately?"

Tony grinned. "Not since this morning."

"I love you," James said, drawing him in with one hand on his belt. "I love you," he murmured, kissing the corner of Tony's mouth. "I love you," he gasped, grinding their hips together.

Tony's boots fell with a clatter to the kitchen tile as he wrapped his arms around his husband. "I missed you today," Tony murmured, sliding his hands into James's back pockets. "Getting that text this morning? All I wanted to do was share my excitement with you."

"You didn't text at all."

"I was visiting today."

"Ah." James swayed them back and forth. "Good?"

"One was. He thought I was cool. Really opened up."

"Didn't know you very well then," James teased.

"Hey, I'll have you know I got moves," Tony replied, a twinkle in his eye. "I pulled the hottest woman *and* man I know. Even managed to get them to marry me."

"Great con," James said playfully. "How'd you swing that?"

"Well, it might have something to do with my magical tongue."

"Oh really?"

"Wanna try it out?"

"Yes," James replied breathlessly.

"Great. Go upstairs and spread the rose petals from the top of the stairs to the bed. If you did a good job, I'll strip you down and show you just how talented my tongue is."

"Fuck, I think I just came a little bit," James said with a chuckle. "Aren't we supposed to be saving our sperm?"

"Don't worry." Tony grinned impishly. "I won't let you come."

"Jesus." James blew out a breath. "Okay." He ran a hand over the back of his neck. "Okay." He left the kitchen.

Tony smirked. It was rare to see James lose his cool like this, and he loved that it was because of him. He turned off the stovetop and moved the sauce off the element, giving it a little stir to make sure none of the hot stuff on the bottom was sticking.

Then he brought his boots down to the front door with the rest of their footwear. There was a shelf and hook in the back entry for his motorcycle equipment like his helmet and jacket, but not his boots, unless he left them on the stairs, which was a trip hazard.

Looking around the narrow front entry, he remembered his words to his spouses about needing to find a more accessible house if they were going to have a baby. It made his heart hurt to think about moving out of this house. They had made it a home. He shook his head at himself. "Getting sentimental over a building," he muttered. "You moved how many times before you were twelve? It's the people who matter."

His little pep talk didn't help much, and he made a mental note to mention it to his spouses and therapist.

Speaking of spouses, he'd given James enough time to get ready upstairs, so he joined him. The path to the bed was beautifully done, and James was waiting for him at the side of the room.

"Perfect," Tony said, stepping over the petals. "You did such a good job."

James visibly brightened at his words, making Tony's heart stutter with joy.

"You asked about my day, but I didn't hear about yours," Tony said, undoing the buttons down the front of James's shirt. "Did your kids behave?"

"There was an incident with a—" James broke off when Tony kissed his sternum.

"Don't let me stop you," Tony teased.

James swallowed hard. "With a water bottle," he continued. "At recess."

"Did their clothes dry in two seconds flat?" Tony asked, nimble fingers making quick work of belt and zipper.

"Oh yeah. Still not allowed."

"Of course not." Tony pushed the pants over James's ass and they fell to the ground with a muffled thump. "What did you do?"

"Made him apologize." James drew in a sharp breath when Tony ran a finger up his length over his cotton briefs. "And write a letter to both sets of parents explaining why what he did was wrong and he wouldn't do it again. His parents have to return it signed tomorrow. Oh *fuck*, Tony."

Tony hummed and continued mouthing along the damp spot on the briefs. "Yes?" he asked, burying his nose in solid muscle and inhaling deeply.

"If you don't put your mouth on me in the next three seconds, I'm going to take matters into my own hands."

"Only three? You're more impatient than usual."

James growled, the sound shooting straight to Tony's cock, and pounced on him, knocking him to the ground. He wrestled Tony's shirt and jeans off, not that Tony was preventing him from doing so.

Once they were both down to their underwear, Tony took control of the situation again, flipping James over onto his hands and knees, and pressing cock against ass, two thin cotton layers too many between them. "You're going to stay in this position for me," Tony said conversationally. "I'm going to get a dam, and then I'm going to eat you until you're begging me to let you come."

"Fuck, Tony," James breathed, his muscles in his back clenching.

Tony yanked James's briefs down under his ass, massaging the round globes with his hands. "Take them off," he ordered, smacking his ass just to watch it jiggle. Then he got up and dug through the end table for a dental dam while watching James struggle to free himself from his underwear, cock bobbing and leaking heavily underneath him. Dam secured, he also grabbed a cock ring before rejoining his lover on the floor.

"You're not going to come until you're buried inside our wife," he murmured, reaching around James and securing the cock ring at the base of his length. Once done, he traced the thick vein on the underside of his cock with a finger, making it jump. "Get it?"

"Got it," James replied thickly.

"Good." Tony ripped open the plastic of the dam. "Spread your knees and hold yourself open for me."

"Oh God," James muttered, pressing the side of his head to the ground so he could reach behind him.

"You will call only my name, not his," Tony ordered.

"Tony," James whimpered.

"That's better," Tony said approvingly, running a finger over puckered skin to watch it twitch. "I can't wait to get my mouth on you." He pressed down, pulling him open.

"Hnng," James groaned.

"I've got you, Jamie," Tony whispered, kissing down the base of his spine while pulling out the dam and laying it out. He dipped his head down and licked from one end to the other.

"Oh fuck."

Tony smirked and circled his tongue around the rim, loosening it enough to spear deep inside.

James shouted wordlessly, his hips jolting forward before pressing back.

Humming, Tony continued fucking into him, flicking the rim on each pull out.

"*Tony*," James moaned, one hand gripping Tony's head to keep him tight against his ass. "Oh *fuck*, I want to come."

Tony chuckled and buried his face harder against the muscle, aiming deep with his tongue, but not quite able to reach the spongy tissue that would make James go wild. "Not yet."

"I knoooow," James groaned.

"Well, *this* is quite the welcome home," Amanda said from the doorway. "Love the rose petals, and the view's not bad either."

"Please get over here," James begged. "I'm not allowed to come unless it's inside you."

"That's positively diabolic," she teased. "What if I'd been home later?"

"I forgot how good it felt," James admitted.

Tony laughed and sucked hard on his rim, making him shout again.

"He was born with a talented mouth," Amanda said, making eye contact with Tony. "Both for getting himself out of trouble and in the bedroom."

Tony smirked against James's ass, plundering it with his tongue.

"I thought maybe you'd want to take me together this first time," Amanda suggested.

"Yes," James panted. "I want that. Tony, *Tony*, I need you to stop or I'm not going to last."

Pulling off with an obscene slurp, Tony sat back on his heels, breathing hard. "Strip for us, darlin'. I want to admire your lingerie up close."

"I thought you'd like it." She slowly stripped off her dark green blouse and cream skirt, letting them flutter down to pool at her feet. "Where do you want me?"

Tony's cock gave a weak twitch. "The edge of the bed. Spread your knees for us."

Amanda shook her blonde hair behind her shoulders and sat in the position he requested, showing the damp spot on her panties.

"How long have you been wet?" James asked, rotating to sit in front of her and running a finger down the dark patch.

"All day," she admitted readily. "Ever since I took the ovulation test this morning. I knew I'd be getting thoroughly fucked tonight."

"Well, you're not wrong," Tony said with a chuckle, cupping her breast in one hand and dragging his thumb over her nipple. "You look so sexy."

"I try," she gasped when James flicked her clit.

"We need to stretch you," Tony murmured. "Are you ready for Jamie to suck on your clit? Give you the first orgasm of the night?"

"Yes," she breathed.

"Up," James ordered, tapping her thigh. "And Tony, you sit. She's going to cockwarm you while I eat her."

"I'm not going to last when she comes," Tony said, shaking his head.

"Yes, you will." James lifted an eyebrow pointedly. "Get a ring and put it on."

"The stretching ring would pull double duty," Amanda suggested.

"Okay, okay." Tony stripped out of his briefs and grabbed the rubber ring. It widened at the base of the cock, which would make it easier to stretch her after she orgasmed. He sat where she had been, admiring her ass while James slowly pulled her panties off.

"Legs apart," James said. "I need room to get at her pussy."

Spreading his knees to make room for his husband between them, Tony's emotions roiled in his chest. He guided his wife onto his cock, her wet warmth almost overwhelming him before the hard pressure of James's shoulders against his thighs made his breath catch in his throat.

Banishing his thoughts to the back of his mind, he focused on the present, on her walls rippling around him and the chin brushing against his sac.

Amanda was still wearing her bra, which was a crime against humanity, and he relieved her of it with a practiced flick of his fingers, tossing it far away, and cupping her breasts with both hands to play with her sensitive nipples.

Her head fell back against his shoulder as her hips made stilted rolls. "Feels so good. I'm going to come like this."

"Yes, you are," Tony murmured in her ear. "You're going to reward Jamie for the hard work he's putting in. Tell him how good he's making you feel."

"James, fuck, you're amazing," she panted. "Your tongue is perfect. James, oh God, *James!*" she whimpered, hips rolling harder. "So close, fuck..."

Tony pinched her nipples lightly and she shattered under the pressure, back arching as she cried out, walls clenching down on his cock.

He gritted his teeth. Even with the dulled sensation and pressure around the base of his cock thanks to the ring, every instinct urged him to rut up into her, to spill inside her. "Jamie," he groaned. "Help."

James chuckled. "You can do it."

"Evil," Tony muttered, trying to count backwards from twenty in his mind. When Amanda sagged on top of him, he breathed a sigh of relief. He hadn't come yet.

"I'm ready for you both," she said weakly.

"We'll see," James said. "Let's get you on your back."

They managed to shift positions until she was lying between them, James and Tony both fingering her open.

"I'm almost scared to take the ring off," Tony said. "The pressure of it feels like the only thing keeping me from exploding."

"You want to give me your cum, don't you?" Amanda asked, blinking up at him. "You won't come until you're inside me."

"Not sure I have the same confidence, but I'll try my best," Tony promised. "You feel like heaven, darlin'."

"I think she can take us," James said. "How do you feel, sunshine? Want to try?"

"Yes, please. I feel like a bowstring that's been pulled back for too long. The tension is going to break me."

"Not sure that metaphor works, but I really don't care at this point," Tony said. "Do you have a preference for position?"

"I think James on bottom, you behind me." She wiggled her body and winked at him. "I know how much you like my ass."

"That I do, darlin'."

"Let's get these rings off," James said, blowing out a sharp breath as his fingers brushed his cock. "I'm on a hair trigger. This isn't going to last long."

"Same."

"Good thing I'm hungry, or I'd be upset," Amanda teased them. "Stuff me full of your cum. Fuck a baby into me."

Tony's breath caught. They'd pretended this scenario in the past, but all of a sudden, it was real. They were actually trying to conceive.

Once more, he pushed his emotions to the back of his mind, focusing on aiming James's cock inside her, and then squeezing in beside him. The tight grip she had on them mirrored the one on his heart.

"Move, Tony," James gritted out.

"Right." He pulled back slowly, the smooth glide helped by copious arousal and lube.

"Fuck us!" Amanda whined.

He slammed back in, and everyone groaned in unison, the best music in the world.

"Fuck yes," James growled.

Tony kept the pace going, twice, three more times, but then pleasure started overwhelming him. "I can't—" he gasped.

"Me too," James panted.

"Clit," Amanda whimpered.

Tony reached underneath her body and flicked over her clit until she shouted her pleasure, walls gripping him so hard his brain shut off. He could feel their cocks pulsing against each other as he came, his mouth open in a silent scream. It wasn't until everyone caught their breath that he realized he had also come.

"Tony, you're crying?" James asked, reaching up and wiping a tear away from his cheek.

"I..." Tony sniffed and dug the heels of his palms against his eyes. "Overwhelmed with love, I think."

"Aww," Amanda cooed. "I want to hug you. Help!"

Chuckling wetly, Tony pulled out of her and she rolled onto her back, arms open to him.

"Hang on, you're leaking," James said, tucking her knees up against her chest.

"Isn't that a myth?" Amanda asked.

"But what if it isn't?" Tony pushed the leaking fluids back inside her pussy.

"I want to cuddle you."

Tony lay beside her, accepting the comfort of her hug.

"Overwhelmed with love?" she whispered, kissing the tip of his nose.

"I never thought I'd make it this far."

"What do you mean?"

Tony sighed. "The kid I visited this morning reminded me of me when I was first adopted by my parents. It brought up a lot of half-buried memories and emotions. And to come home to this house—our home—bursting with love..." He took a shaky breath and felt tears slip from his eyes again. "We're trying to create a new life together. This baby is going to grow up *so* loved. It's beyond my wildest dreams, even though we've been talking about it for years now."

James took a position behind him, spooning their bodies together, and dropped a kiss on his shoulder. "We are lucky to have you in our lives."

"A lot of things had to fall into place in order for me to have arrived in Northampton when I did," Tony admitted. "Not all of them good."

"I'm sorry," Amanda said sadly.

"I didn't mean to bring the mood down," Tony said, giving himself a shake.

"You didn't," James reassured him.

"In that case, I'm also sad that we're going to have to sell this place and move," Tony said.

Amanda giggled. "That's getting a little ahead of ourselves. We don't need to worry about accessibility until I'm pregnant."

Tony ran a hand over her belly, reveling in the softness of her skin. "You could be pregnant right now," he marvelled. "And we won't know for another few weeks."

"At least."

"We should probably keep trying, just to make sure it sticks," James teased.

Tony chuckled. "Oh yeah, totally."

"You are positively glowing!" Amanda's mom cooed at her the second they entered the house at Christmas.

"Thanks, Mom," Amanda said, shrugging out of her light jacket. "I feel like I'm in a constant state of overheating, so I think that's just sweat."

"I've got the luggage," Tony said, placing it off to the side. "I wanted to make sure she didn't slip on any black ice on the way up to the door."

"It hasn't been cold enough for ice yet," Amanda's dad said.

"I tried to tell him that," Amanda said, smiling fondly at her husband. "They're both being extra cautious with me."

"As they should be." Julie took her daughter's hand. "Your room is all set up with clean sheets, and we pushed the beds together for you."

"Aww, thanks Mom." Amanda kissed her cheek. "When will the others get here?"

"Michael left for the airport about an hour ago. They'll want to settle in with the kids, so they'll come over just before dinner. Ava and Xavier are waiting for our text."

James knocked on the door just then, and they moved out of the way for his bags and parcels. "My parents are right behind me. They saw us arrive."

"I guess you don't need to text," Tony said with a chuckle, kneeling to help Amanda take off her boots. "They're not eager to see their grandbump or anything."

"We're all extremely excited about the pregnancy," Julie said. "Can I touch?"

Amanda shrugged. "Sure, but I haven't felt any movement or anything yet."

"Doesn't matter. Just knowing that my grandchild is in here is enough." Julie wiped at her eyes with her free hand, the other on Amanda's belly. "Have you found out the sex yet?"

"We're going to let it be a surprise."

"But how will we buy clothes for them?"

Amanda laughed. "There are plenty of options. Also, we expect they'll be in pyjamas most of the time."

"But there are so many cute onesies!"

"Then buy them," Tony said with a shrug. "We're going with the flow."

"What about names?"

James rolled his eyes at the other two and they all chuckled. "We're keeping that a secret too."

"But—"

"Dear, we'll find out in about four months," Paul said.

"But what if they pick a name I hate?" Julie said with a pout.

"Then you won't say anything because the baby will already be named," James said, an edge to his tone.

"Careful, your protective side is showing," Amanda teased him.

"Let your parents in," Tony said, opening the door. "We're moving out of the entryway now," he said to them.

"Merry Christmas!" they greeted each other.

"Where is my daughter?" Ava said, reaching for Amanda and pulling her into a hug before even taking off her boots. "How are you? Are you eating better now?"

Amanda made a face. "Somewhat. Thank you for your suggestion to have the boys cook the meat when I'm out of the house. I've managed to stomach more since we started that."

"I'm so glad you have someone you can call for questions like that," Julie said.

"I didn't call, actually. I didn't think of it," Amanda said sheepishly.

"I did," Tony said. "I was worried. She'd eat two bites and then say she was full."

"That's an exaggeration, I hope?" Julie asked.

"Sadly, no." James frowned. "I'm glad Tony took the initiative."

"Yeah, now I can eat five bites," Amanda teased.

"Unless it's watermelon," Tony teased.

"Oh yeah. Do we have any?" she asked hopefully, perking up.

"If not, I'll go get some," Tony said.

"We don't," Julie said.

"I'll go with you," Xavier offered.

"Great." Tony grinned at his father-in-law. "Hopefully watermelon is cheaper here than in Boston."

"It's the middle of winter, it's expensive everywhere," James said dryly.

"Sorry," Amanda said in a small voice.

"You're not eating much else. It's completely worth it," Tony said, kissing her temple. He gently brushed a hand over her belly. She wasn't showing much, but it was enough that he could feel the difference.

Later that evening, when the trio were getting ready for bed, James pulled a Santa hat out of their suitcase and tossed it to Tony, who caught it one-handed.

"What's that for?" Amanda asked.

Tony put it on his head and sat on the bed. "Ho ho ho," he said cheerfully. "What would you like for Christmas, young lady?"

"Young lady?" she giggled. "I'm thirty!"

"And I'm Santa Claus." Tony winked at her. "Want to sit on my lap and tell me your Christmas list?"

Mirth dancing in her eyes, she glanced down at his hard cock. "Why yes, Santa. That sounds delightful." She slid onto his lap, throwing her head back onto his shoulder as she took him inside her body. "Best part of being pregnant," she gasped.

"More blood in your body means higher sensitivity," James said, placing a matching Santa hat on his own head.

She reached for him, pulling him to her by his cock. "I've always wanted to be spit-roasted by Santa."

"Didn't we do that last year?" Tony asked.

"No, you double-stuffed me."

"Ah."

"Besides," she licked up the underside of James's cock, "I've never had two Santas while pregnant."

"That's true." Tony kissed the back of her neck. "Can I have some of that Santa sausage?"

James groaned. "I thought the point of this position was so that she wouldn't be overheard when she comes?"

"I'll let her take you down her throat when she's close to coming," Tony said. "But in the meantime, I want a share."

Amanda held the cock out for him. "The more the merrier."

Tony sucked the head into his mouth eagerly, and was rewarded with a spurt of pre-cum on his tongue. His cock twitched within Amanda, and she whimpered.

"You need to come, sunshine?" James asked her.

"Yes," she gasped.

"Santa, this young lady has been a very good girl. Why don't you give her an early Christmas present?" James suggested.

Tony's fingers danced across her belly and down between her legs, tracing where he was splitting her open before narrowing in on her clit. It took two gentle flicks before she moaned loudly, and he popped off James's cock.

She took him in her mouth, bobbing her head a couple times before pulling back to suckle on the crown when she came.

Her walls clamped down hard on Tony, making his eyes roll back in his head. "Fuck, darlin'," he groaned under his breath.

She panted, letting James drop from her lips. "Thank you for my gift, Santa."

"We're not half done with you yet, sunshine," James promised.

"You've been an extra good girl this year," Tony continued.

Amanda giggled quietly. "Merry Christmas to me."

Tony got up from the chair beside the delivery room bed and stretched, his back popping twice in a row, and grimaced. The room was quiet, the slight beeping of the machines a dull background noise.

After the epidural was given, Amanda had fallen asleep.

That was hours ago, and though the nurse had checked on her several times, there was nothing for him or James to do but wait.

James was stretched out on the 'comfy' chair in the corner, his head leaning against the wall and legs splayed out.

Tony snorted softly. It did *not* look comfortable.

The nurse barely spared him a glance as he left the room. He double checked the number to make sure it was fresh in his mind before heading down the hall.

A woman screamed through her delivery a couple doors down, and he sent mental good wishes to her as he walked past her room.

The hospital delivery waiting room was quiet at this hour of the night. Tony used the bathroom, grabbed a coffee from the complimentary cart, and headed back to the room.

Everyone was just as he had left them. He wandered over to the side of the bed with the machines and bent over the chart that was tracking her contractions.

"She's progressing well," the nurse whispered. "I'm estimating another half hour at most."

"And then what?"

"And then she'll be able to start pushing."

Tony's heart leapt, a mix of excitement and anxiety rushing through him. He glanced at the peacefully sleeping Amanda. A curl of hair had fallen over her face and he gently pushed it behind her ear. "Looking forward to it."

He tried his best to not look at the clock every two seconds, but the wait seemed interminable. Half an hour had never seemed so long.

Finally, the nurse gently shook Amanda's shoulder. "Time to wake up," she said. "Do you feel like you need to push?"

Amanda drowsily twisted half onto her back. "Ummm…"

"Like you need to poop."

"Yeah, I guess I do," Amanda replied slowly. "It feels really weird. Tony?"

"I'm here. What do you need?"

"The baby's coming," she said calmly, at odds with her words and wide eyes. "Can we do this?"

"Hell yeah, we can," Tony said, squeezing her hand. "The three of us can handle anything."

Amanda nodded. "You're right."

"I need you to roll onto your back now," the nurse instructed, getting ready to help her.

"I'm going to wake James," Tony said, kissing her temple.

"Please," she said. Then she gripped his hand. "Hang on…" She took several deep breaths, eyes unfocused on the center of his shirt. "Okay, now you can go."

That she'd needed him in the middle of a contraction had made him feel ten feet tall. "James," he whispered, shaking his husband's shoulder gently.

"Hmm?" James muttered sleepily, eyes half lidded. Then they snapped open. "It's time?"

"It is."

A beaming smile broke across his face, and Tony fell a little bit more in love with him. "Let's go support our wife."

Tony pulled him to his feet and they exchanged a quick kiss before returning to the delivery bed. "Where can we stand that's out of your way?" he asked the nurse.

"I want each of you holding a leg. You're going to help her pull her legs in, towards her belly, on each push. Each push is a count of five. We're going to try for three pushes with each contraction. Are you ready?"

"I pull my legs *in*?" Amanda asked, drowsily confused. "I thought I would push."

"No." The nurse smiled at her. "Pulling in puts more force on your pushing muscles. Here we go!"

The next hour was a blur to Tony. He supported Amanda as she labored, sweat glistening on her face and her hair in disarray. She'd never looked more beautiful. Every so often, he'd glance over at James, mirroring him on her left side, and they'd nod at each other.

We've got this, he seemed to say.

A doctor came in at one point, checked on her, and disappeared again. She came back after a while, nodded, and pulled on gloves. "The baby's almost here, Amanda. You're going to push harder than you ever have before."

Amanda's eyes widened. "I have been," she whispered.

Tony gripped her hand. "I believe in you," he said.

"You're amazing," James added.

She took a deep breath and nodded, setting her jaw.

"Push!" the doctor ordered.

"Gyah!" Amanda cried, tears trickling down her face.

"Again!"

"I can't!" Amanda gasped. "Tony, tell her I can't!"

"Darlin', you can," he said. "You want to be pregnant for the rest of your life?"

Amanda huffed a laugh.

"Push," the doctor urged.

"Argh!" Amanda screamed, nearly breaking Tony's fingers with her grip.

A gush of fluid heralded the arrival. The doctor caught the baby deftly, placing it on Amanda's belly. "There you go," she said, rubbing the baby's back until it let out a cry. "A healthy baby girl."

"A girl," Tony repeated shakily. "We have a daughter?"

"We do." James let go of Amanda's leg and pressed their foreheads together. "You're a superhero," he murmured to her. "I'm so proud of you."

"She's okay?" Amanda asked.

"See for yourself," Tony said, wiping tears away from his cheeks.

Amanda ran a light finger over the baby's wet head. "She's perfect."

"I never had any doubts." Tony swooped down to kiss her gently. "I didn't think I could love you more," he whispered.

"We're going to clean her and weigh her now. Who would like to cut the cord?"

"We've worked it out," Tony said, reaching for the scissors.

James put his hand on Tony's, guiding him, and they cut the cord together.

"I'm going to get a picture of her," James said, following the nurse with the baby over to the corner.

Amanda closed her eyes and rested her head, legs still splayed apart. "I'm so tired," she mumbled.

"You have to deliver the placenta," the doctor said.

"Can she have a break first?" Tony asked, gently brushing the hair off Amanda's face.

The doctor checked the vitals. "Five minutes."

Tony hooked his chair with an ankle and sat, leaning his head next to Amanda's. "Rest, darlin'. You're almost done."

"Why didn't they warn us about this part in the baby class?" Amanda said with a tiny whimper.

Tony shrugged. "Maybe it's forgettable?"

"I have a question."

He raised an eyebrow.

"You'll tell me the truth, right?"

"I am not in the habit of lying."

"Did I poop?" she asked, flushing.

Tony hid a smile with a hand. "You went on the toilet before the epidur-al, remember? There was no poop while you were laboring. But you know that even if you had, it's completely normal, right?"

"I know," she said. "I do. I'm still glad I didn't."

"Here you go. One clean baby. She's seven pounds, ten ounces, and twenty-two inches." The nurse deposited the baby on Amanda's chest.

"Oh, hello little one," Amanda cooed at the baby.

She lifted her head up and looked straight at Tony, her eyes so dark blue that the pupil seemed too big.

"That's your Papi," Amanda said, smiling at him.

Tony kissed her lips and then the baby's tiny forehead.

She put her head down for only a second before lifting it again, this time looking over to the other side, where James was sitting.

"And that's your Daddy," Amanda continued, a silent tear escaping her eye.

Tony caught it with the back of his finger before brushing her hair back off her forehead.

The baby put her head down again, making the cutest yawn sound he'd ever heard in his life.

"She has your nose," James said to him, gently rubbing his finger down the baby's cheek.

"How? She has your chin," Tony replied, confused.

"We can do genetic testing—" the nurse began.

"No!

"Not necessary."

"No, thank you."

The three of them spoke at once, their voices overlapping in their hurry to deny the offer.

"Alright, I need the attention of the mother, please," the doctor said. "One of you, please take the baby. You can do skin-to-skin."

"I'll stay with Amanda," James said. "You take her first."

Tony nodded, whipping off his shirt and carefully picking up the tiny baby.

She protested once, but settled against him when he draped a blanket over her. Her tiny hand wiggled against his skin, a slight tickle that from anyone else would make him bat them away. "You've already got me wrapped around your finger," he whispered to her. "Your Daddy too, if I know him."

She yawned again, and his heart melted. "I love you," he murmured, running his fingers gently down her back, the newborn fuzz so soft.

He felt a little guilty about not being there for Amanda as she labored the afterbirth, but it was hard not to revel in the tiny form asleep on his chest. *I helped make her,* he thought in awe. *I'm her Papi!*

Unbidden, tears came into his eyes again. He blinked furiously, trying to will them away.

James squatted down in front of him. "Everything good, cowboy?"

"Overwhelmed," Tony croaked. He spared a quick glance over James's head. Amanda was asleep again, the doctor nowhere to be seen. "Is she okay?"

"Tired out. The nurse said she'll need to try to walk to the bathroom when she wakes up, but she can sleep for a bit."

Tony nodded. "You should hold the baby."

A flicker of panic crossed James's face.

"Take off your shirt," Tony said, taking charge. There was no way he was going to let James be afraid to hold his—their—daughter. He got smoothly to his feet and James took his place, sitting rigidly. The transfer to the new body was swift, the baby not doing more than letting out a sleepy wheeze before rubbing her face on James's chest. "She's got that newborn scrunch, so you can easily support her by her butt. Just let her get used to your heartbeat. Talk to her a bit. I'm right here."

The tension left James's shoulders slowly. "Look at her hair," he murmured. "There's so much of it!"

"No wonder Amanda had heartburn," Tony said.

"I thought that was a myth."

Tony shrugged. "Seems to be proven right with this one."

"Her fingers are so little," James marveled. "So perfect."

"Tony?" Amanda said weakly from the bed.

He whirled around. "What's up?"

"I need to pee. Can you help me?"

"Of course."

He tried not to blanch at the amount of blood left behind in the toilet and took heart from the strength of Amanda's grip on his arm.

Once they were back in the room and Amanda relaxed on the bed again, James gave the baby to her to cuddle.

"What are we going to name her?" Amanda asked, playing with a tiny black curl.

Exchanging a glance with James, Tony said, "Lily."

James nodded. "Lily Beatrice."

"Oh." Amanda's eyes filled with tears. "For Grandmother."

"We know how much you loved her. She would be overjoyed to meet this little one," James said. "The next best thing was to name her after her."

"And her favorite flower," Tony added. "Do you like it?"

"I love it. I knew you two would pick the perfect name." Amanda looked down at the sleeping little girl. "Hello, Lily Beatrice. Welcome to the world. We can't wait to show it to you."

Acknowledgements

Thank you to my husband for continuously telling me that I'm doing a good job and tightening up the beginnings of my chapters.

I would also like to thank pinkpiggy93 for creating the beautiful cover art on all three books in this series. She was a pleasure to work with.

I would like to acknowledge that this book was written on the unceded, unsurrendered Territory of the Anishinaabe Algonquin Nation, and I pay our respects to elders both past and present.

It is unbelievable to me that this series is complete. I started writing it, or rather, a scene of it, way back in 2011. It has morphed since then and really grown into itself. I am so proud of what I've accomplished, and I couldn't have done this without Geneva at River City Siren Press, who believed in my book and characters before they were even fully written. Thank you!!

www.ingramcontent.com/pod-product-compliance
Lightning Source LLC
Chambersburg PA
CBHW022120050726
47591CB00002B/858